Fax: 020 7641 0000

Northanger Abbey

Original story by Jane Austen
Retold by Rebecca Stevens
Series Advisor Professor Kimberley Reynolds
Illustrated by Davide Ortu

OXFORD
UNIVERSITY PRESS

Letter from the Author

When I was growing up, I went to a small primary school where my mum was one of the teachers. She taught me in the top class and whenever the room got noisy she used to shout, 'Rebecca Stevens! I won't tell you again!' – even though it wasn't always me who was talking. I didn't mind, though. I knew she was only doing it so the other children didn't think I got special treatment because she was my mum.

I don't remember much that Mum taught us, but I do remember one thing: she loved stories. She loved making them up and reading them – to us and to herself. Her favourite book was *Northanger Abbey*. I didn't read it until I was older but when I did, I loved it too. Catherine, the central character, didn't seem like a girl from another century. She seemed like me: a girl who loved reading and longed to get away from the small village where she grew up to have adventures – and who would be so pleased to know that one day she would be the heroine in a book of her own!

Rebecca Stevens

The World of *Northanger Abbey*

Northanger Abbey is a story about stories. Catherine, the central character, imagines herself as the romantic heroine in a novel, who'll fall in love, get married and live happily ever after. But real life wasn't like that. In Jane Austen's time, marriage was usually as much about money as it was about love. If you met somebody and fell in love, you'd need your father's permission before you could marry, and that would normally depend on how much money each family had.

But this didn't stop people from dreaming and wishing things were different. When Jane Austen wrote *Northanger Abbey* in 1798–99, readers had recently discovered a new form of fiction. It was usually romantic, sometimes scary and always exciting, and because the stories were often set in spooky castles with Gothic architecture,[1] it became known as Gothic fiction. The book Catherine reads – *The Mysteries of Udolpho* by Ann Radcliffe – was one of the most popular of these novels, selling far more copies than any of Jane Austen's books at the time.

Gothic novels were incredibly popular – especially among young women and girls – but not everyone approved of them, considering them overdramatic and somehow 'improper'. Jane Austen makes fun of gothic

---

[1] Gothic architecture is characterized by tall spires, high vaulted ceilings and windows with pointed arches.

novels in *Northanger Abbey* – though I think she secretly liked them!

I wonder what she would think if she knew that her 'little work' (as she called *Northanger Abbey*) would be so well-loved and would sell even better in the end than *The Mysteries of Udolpho* itself!

Cast of Characters

James Morland
Also known as: Mr Morland
Catherine's brother

Catherine Morland
Also known as: Miss Morland
Our heroine

Mrs Allen
A friend of the Morland
family and Catherine's
chaperone in Bath

John Thorpe
Also known as: Mr Thorpe
Isabella's brother

Isabella Thorpe
Also known as: Miss Thorpe
Catherine's friend

Note

In Jane Austen's time, you would only have called people by their first names if they were very close friends or family. It was considered polite to refer to everyone else by their title, for example: Miss Morland, Mr Thorpe, Captain Tilney.

General Tilney
Henry's father

Henry Tilney
Also known as: Mr Tilney

Frederick Tilney
Also known as:
Captain Tilney
Henry's older brother

Eleanor Tilney
Also known as: Miss Tilney
Henry's sister

8

Part 1

Chapter 1
Catherine

Nobody would ever write a book about Catherine Morland. She was not that sort of girl. She grew up in Fullerton, a small village in the middle of nowhere, in an ordinary family, not rich and not poor, with an ordinary mother and an ordinary father and a great many ordinary brothers and sisters.

But Catherine did not want to be ordinary. She wanted to be a heroine.

It was a large family, with ten children, so Catherine's mother was always busy with the little ones and her father generally occupied with his work. Catherine was the eldest girl, with three older brothers, so when she was very young she had always preferred games like cricket and climbing trees to playing with dolls and picking flowers. As a little girl she had been rather thin and very pale, with straight dark hair that hung around her face like string; the kind of child who loved nothing better than rolling down the green slope at the back of the house with her brothers and always seemed to have dirt under her fingernails. She was not particularly pretty or especially clever, had never liked drawing or any of the other things young girls were supposed to enjoy, and the day her mother gave up trying to teach her to play the piano had been one of the happiest of her life.

But then, as she grew older, Catherine began to change. Her love of dirt gave way to a liking for fine clothes, and she was pleased one day to hear her mother remark to her father that 'Catherine grows into quite a good-looking girl – she is almost pretty today'. To be almost pretty, for a girl who had been seen as definitely ordinary for the first fifteen years of her life, was high praise indeed.

She also discovered reading. It was between the ages of fifteen and seventeen that Catherine was in training to be a heroine, so she read all such works as a heroine must to prepare herself for the role. She studied poetry, and the plays of Shakespeare, and gained much useful information about tragic queens and doomed love affairs, but very little about where a young heroine might happen to meet her hero or what she should be wearing at the time. For this, she turned to novels. These were not the kind of books her father wanted her to read, full of facts and dates and historical information – they were stories. Delightful stories with names like *The Castle of Otranto* and *Horrid Mysteries*, full of beautiful heroines and handsome heroes, cruel husbands and neglected wives locked up in ghost-infested castles in distant lands, full of gloomy passages and candle-lit bedchambers with portraits of long-dead ancestors whose eyes followed you around the room, with ancient chests packed with secrets and mysterious locked doors through which you were forbidden to pass ...

But although Catherine longed to be like one of the heroines in her stories, she had managed to reach the great age of seventeen without having had even one adventure. She had never stayed in a crumbling castle or visited an ancient palace in a foreign land. She had never been beyond her village, in fact, except to go shopping with her mother in Salisbury – and that was only nine miles away. She had not met one young man who brought a blush to her cheeks and had never herself inspired anything more than mild admiration in the red-faced son of a local farmer who lived nearby. There was not one lord in the village – no, not even a baronet; not one family who had brought up as their own a boy accidentally found at their door as a baby; not one young man of unknown origin whom Catherine might accidentally encounter when out for her daily walk.

There were, in fact, no handsome young men in the entire neighbourhood, no romantic poets or wicked princes, no dances, no excitement, no mysteries, no fun. Catherine would never be like the girls she read about. She would never meet a hero, never have an adventure, never be the heroine of her own story. Nobody would ever write a book about her and nothing would ever change.

But, when a young lady is to be a heroine, the limitations of one small village in Wiltshire cannot prevent her.

Something must and will happen to throw a hero in her way.

* * *

Mr and Mrs Allen were friends of Catherine's parents who lived in Fullerton. They were a wealthy couple – kind, if a little dull – who had no children of their own and always spent several weeks of the year in Bath, a large town where people went to talk and to dance, make friends and have fun.

And this year, the year Catherine was seventeen, the Allens invited her to go with them. Catherine's life as the romantic heroine of her own story had begun.

Chapter 2
The First Ball

Catherine was determined to be happy. This was the beginning of her adventure, the beginning of her new life, and she was going to enjoy it.

But the journey did not start well.

Her mother did not behave at all like a mother should when her eldest daughter leaves home for the first time. There were no floods of tears or solemn words of warning about the terrible dangers that could face a young lady who is going out into the world on her own. She just told Catherine to wrap herself up warm when she went out at night and keep an account of everything she spent.

Her sister Sarah was also a disappointment. She did not beg Catherine to write every day, describing every detail of everything she saw and everyone she met. She just gave her a quick kiss and went back to reading her book. And then there was their father, who completely failed to give Catherine unlimited access to his bank account or press a hundred-pound note into her hand, promising her more whenever she needed it. He gave her ten guineas and told her not to spend it all at once.

The journey was also sadly uneventful. The Allens' carriage was not overturned in a flood or attacked by robbers, which made it completely unnecessary for them to be rescued by any handsome young men on horseback. The most disturbing thing to happen was when Mrs Allen thought she might have left her bag in the inn where they stopped for lunch. And even this turned out to be a false alarm.

But when they had arrived in Bath and were driving through the streets of the city to their lodgings, Catherine forgot about the uneventful journey and her family's disappointing farewells. The city looked so fine and the streets were so busy! She had come to Bath to be happy and she felt happy already. She was away from home, and soon she would be going to her first ball!

* * *

But first, there was shopping to be done. Mrs Allen was not the most brilliant or accomplished of women, but she was in one way the perfect companion for a young lady who was just going out in the world. Mrs Allen loved clothes. She had a most harmless delight in dressing up, and our heroine was not to be allowed out in public until she had been provided with a gown of the latest fashion and hair that was newly cut and styled. Only then did Mrs Allen declare that Catherine looked 'quite as she should do' and they could venture out to the ball.

'I wish you could dance, my dear,' said Mrs Allen. 'I wish you could get a partner.'

Mrs Allen had been so long in dressing that they had not got to the Upper Rooms (where the ball was taking place) till late. The ballroom was terribly crowded and Mr Allen had immediately gone off to play cards in another room, leaving the two ladies to squeeze in as well as they could, until they found some seats at the side of the room. Catherine longed to dance, she longed to join in, but they did not know anybody. There was not one person with whom they could pass the time. Not one young man who would ask Catherine to dance.

'How uncomfortable it is, Mrs Allen,' whispered Catherine, 'not to know one single person here.'

'Yes, my dear,' Mrs Allen replied, with perfect serenity. 'It is very uncomfortable indeed. How does my gown look? I'm afraid it got a little tumbled in the crowd.'

'It looks very nice. But, dear Mrs Allen, are you sure there is nobody you know among all these people? I think you must know *somebody.*'

'I don't, upon my word. I wish I did. Oh, look! There goes a strange-looking woman! What an odd gown she has on! So old-fashioned! Look at the back!' She patted

Catherine's hand. 'I do wish you could dance, my dear,' she said again. 'I wish you could get a partner.'

She had said it so many times that Catherine could no longer smile in response. How could she dance without a partner and how could she get a partner when they knew nobody in the room?

And then, just when Catherine had begun to wish she could go home to Fullerton and forget that she had ever dreamed of being a heroine, they were approached by the Master of Ceremonies. He had a gentleman with him, a tall young man with a pleasant face, who, if not quite handsome, was very near it. He was introduced to them as Mr Tilney. And he asked Catherine to dance.

'I have been rather remiss, madam,' he said, when they were sitting down afterwards in a quiet corner, 'in paying you the proper attentions of a dance partner.' Catherine looked at him, unsure of whether he was serious. 'I have not asked you all the usual questions,' he continued. 'How long you have been in the city, whether you have been here before, how you like the place, et cetera, et cetera, et cetera.'

Catherine smiled. 'Oh! Pray do not give yourself the trouble, sir!' she said, trying not to laugh.

'But I insist!' Mr Tilney formed his features into a set smile and continued in a simpering voice: 'And have you been long in Bath, madam?'

'Oh! Just a few days, sir!'

'Really!' he replied, with false astonishment. 'Just a few! And how do you find it, may I ask? Are you altogether pleased with the city?'

'I am, sir! I like it very well!'

Mr Tilney went back to his own voice. 'Now I must give one more smirk and we can go back to being normal.'

'I am very glad of it,' said Catherine. And this time she allowed herself to laugh.

Mr Tilney pretended to be offended. He sighed dramatically. 'I see what you think of me,' he said. 'I know what you will write about me in your diary tomorrow!'

'My diary!' Catherine had never kept a diary in her life, but she was not going to tell him that. 'Why? What will I write?'

Mr Tilney thought for a moment. '"Friday",' he said, sucking an imaginary pencil. '"Went to ball. Wore my new muslin robe – white, with blue trimmings – plain black shoes – received many admiring looks but was harassed by a strange man who made me dance with him and distressed me with his nonsense."'

'I shall say no such thing!'

He laughed, then grew serious. 'Shall I tell you what you ought to say, Miss Morland?'

Catherine nodded.

'"Danced with a very agreeable young man who seems to be a most extraordinary genius, and I hope I may know more of him in the future." Mr Tilney looked at her for a long moment. 'That, madam, is what I wish you would say.'

Catherine felt her cheeks grow hot, and found herself unable to look at him. Because that, if she had been the kind of girl who kept a diary, would have been exactly what she would have said.

Chapter 3
A New Friend

'What a delightful place Bath is, my dear.' It was the following morning and our heroine was in the Pump Room with Mrs Allen, who was looking around at the crowds as she spoke. 'And how pleasant it would be if we knew anyone!'

Everyone gathered in the Pump Room during the day to meet, drink tea and admire each other's clothes. Catherine had been so sure they would see Mr Tilney that she had been practising her smile ever since breakfast. But no smile was needed. Everyone in Bath seemed to be there, crowds of people passed in and out, people whom nobody cared about and nobody wanted to see, but Mr Tilney did not appear. Mrs Allen and Catherine were forced to sit at the end of a table without anything to do or anybody to speak to except each other.

'The Skinners were here last year,' said Mrs Allen. 'How I wish they were here now.'

'Dear Mrs Allen, had we better not sit somewhere else? The gentlemen and ladies at this table look as if they are wondering why we came here – we seem to be forcing ourselves into their party.'

'Aye, we do. It is very disagreeable. Oh! Do look at that woman, my dear. What an odd hat she is wearing!

I would not be seen in public with such a thing on my head!'

Catherine was about to reply, when a lady of about Mrs Allen's age approached them.

'I think, madam, I cannot be mistaken,' she said. 'It is a long time since I had the pleasure of seeing you, but is not your name Allen?'

Mrs Allen immediately recognized Mrs Thorpe, an old friend from her school days. The two ladies' joy at meeting again was very great and when they had observed several times how many years had passed since they were last together, what a pleasure it was to see an old friend and how very surprised they were to meet in Bath, they proceeded to exchange information about their families, each lady talking a great deal about herself and barely listening to the other. Mrs Thorpe had one great advantage over her friend as she had acquired a large number of children since they last met and so was able to describe their talents and beauty in great detail. There was John, who was so clever – he was away at university in Oxford; William – so manly – was at sea; and then there were several daughters, each more lovely and accomplished than the last. Poor Mrs Allen, having no children, had no such information to share, and had to console herself with the fact that the lace on Mrs Thorpe's dress was not half as expensive or handsome as her own.

'And here they are!' cried Mrs Thorpe, as three smart-looking young ladies approached, arm in arm. 'Here come my dear girls!' She turned to Mrs Allen and said in an undertone: 'The tallest is Isabella, my eldest. Is she not a fine young woman? The others are much admired too, but I believe Isabella to be the handsomest.'

'How excessively like her brother Miss Morland is!' cried the eldest Miss Thorpe, when they had all been introduced. She was a few years older than Catherine, very graceful and elegant, and dressed in the latest fashion. Catherine thought her the most beautiful creature she had ever seen.

The other Miss Thorpes responded with a chorus of agreement. 'The very picture of him indeed!' and 'I should have known her anywhere for his sister!' was repeated by them all, two or three times.

Catherine was puzzled for a moment, but then she remembered that her eldest brother James had recently made friends with a young man at university whose name was John Thorpe. James had spent the last week of the Christmas holidays with this friend's family and had come home full of stories about John's sister, a girl of exceptional beauty and refinement, he said, whom he hoped his family would meet one day.

So Isabella was this sister – the one James liked so much! It was the most natural thing in the world that she and Catherine would become best friends.

* * *

Over the next few days, the two young ladies spent every spare moment together, getting to know each other better with every passing hour. They called each other by their first names, were always arm in arm when they walked and, if a rainy morning deprived them of their daily outing, they stayed inside and read novels together. Yes, novels! Catherine was delighted to discover that as well as being so elegant and refined, her new friend loved reading novels almost as much as she did.

'My dearest Catherine,' cried Isabella, as our heroine entered the Pump Room one morning, 'what can have made you so late?' (Catherine had arrived a full five minutes after her friend.) 'Have you been reading *Udolpho*?'

The Mysteries of Udolpho was a new book that Isabella had lent her. It was full of horrid scenes of haunted castles and secret passages and bloodstained flagstones. Catherine was enjoying it immensely.

'Yes!' she replied. 'I have got to the part with the black veil!'

'Have you indeed? How delightful! Oh! I would not tell you for the world what is behind the black veil! But are you not wild to know?'

'Do not tell me! I know it must be a skeleton!' Catherine looked at her friend. 'Is it a skeleton, Isabella? Oh, no, no, do not tell me!'

But Isabella's attention was elsewhere. 'For goodness' sake!' she said. 'Let us move away from this end of the room. There are two odious young men who have been staring at me this half-hour!'

'What? Where? I cannot see anyone.'

'Come, let us go and look at the Visitors' Book. They will hardly follow us there.'

Away they walked to the book, which Isabella studied with elaborate care.

'They are not coming this way, are they?' she said. 'I hope they are not so rude as to follow us. Pray let me know if they are coming, Catherine. I am determined I will not look up.'

Catherine assured her that she need not be uneasy. They were quite safe. The two alarming young gentlemen had just left the Pump Room.

'Which way did they go?' said Isabella. 'Oh! I am not going to look!'

'They went towards the church.'

'Well, I am very glad to be rid of them.' Isabella glanced up and down the street. 'Though one was a very good-looking young man. What say we go along to the shop in Milsom Street, Catherine? I can show you the hat I was telling you about.'

'But if we go that way, we may overtake the two young men you were trying to avoid.'

'Oh! I am not concerned about that! I would not flatter them by seeming to care enough to try and avoid them. Come along!'

And so the two young ladies set off as fast as they could in pursuit of the two young men.

Chapter 4
A Surprise!

'Oh, these odious carriages!' said Isabella. 'How I detest them! Do you not detest them, Catherine? I detest them more than anything in the world!'

It was a few days later, and the two friends were out for their morning walk. Catherine had been hoping to come upon Mr Tilney, but he was nowhere to be found. She had not seen him since that night at the ball and every search for him had been unsuccessful. *He must be gone from Bath,* she thought, *although he had not mentioned that his stay would be so brief.* It was most strange. This sort of mysterious disappearance, which is always so attractive in a hero, only increased Catherine's anxiety to know him better and was a subject she often discussed with her new friend.

Isabella was quite sure that Mr Tilney must be a charming young man who was delighted with her dearest Catherine and would return very soon, but in the meantime she had more important things on her mind.

'By the by,' she said, as she watched a young man ride past on a particularly fine-looking horse, 'though I have thought of it a hundred times, I have always forgotten to ask: what is your favourite appearance in a man? Do you prefer them dark or fair?'

'I hardly know,' said Catherine. 'I never much thought of it. Something between both, I suppose. Brown hair, I think – not fair and not very dark.'

'Yes, yes, Catherine, I know. I have not forgotten your description of Mr Tilney!' Catherine blushed and tried to protest, but Isabella continued. 'My taste is different,' she declared. 'I prefer light eyes in a man, and fair hair.' She cast a quick look at Catherine from the corner of her eye. 'Oh! But you must promise not to betray me, my dearest friend! If you should *happen to know* a gentleman of that description ... '

Catherine was puzzled. 'Betray you, Isabella? Whatever do you mean?'

'No, no!' said Isabella. 'I have already said too much! Let us drop the subject.'

Catherine, in some amazement, complied, and after staying silent for a few moments, was on the point of bringing the subject back to Mr Tilney's mysterious disappearance, when her friend stopped her with a sudden cry.

'Catherine, look!' she said. 'Can it be? In that carriage – my brother John and ... ' – she checked her reflection in a shop window and patted her hair – *'Mr Morland!'*

'James? It cannot be!'

The carriage had drawn up opposite them on the other side of the road. Two gentlemen jumped out and Catherine found her hands firmly grasped and her cheeks warmly kissed.

'Catherine!'

'James!' Her eyes danced over her brother's face. As much as she now loved Bath it was delightful to see his familiar smile. 'What are you doing here?'

While Isabella's brother dealt with the horse, greetings were exchanged amongst the three other young people, and James explained how he and his friend had driven to Bath in order to stay with Isabella's family. Had Catherine been a little less delighted and surprised at the meeting she might have noticed the brightness of her friend's eyes and the smiles with which she greeted James. Had she also been more of an expert in other people's feelings and less engrossed in her own, she might also have noticed that her brother thought her friend quite as pretty as she did herself.

'What's this, Morland? Your sister, hey?'

Isabella's brother was a stout young man of middling height with a red face. He carelessly shook his sister's hand and bowed briefly to Catherine, before taking out his pocket watch.

'How long d'you think it took us to drive from Tetbury, Miss Morland?' he said. 'Hey?'

'I fear I could not say, Mr Thorpe,' said Catherine. 'I do not know the distance.'

Her brother informed her it was twenty-three miles.

'Twenty-three!' cried John. 'Have you taken leave of your senses, Morland? It is twenty-five if it is an inch!' He held up his watch. 'It is now half past one. We started from Tetbury as the town clock struck eleven and I defy any man in England to make my horse go less than ten miles an hour!'

'You have lost an hour, John,' said James. 'It was only ten o'clock when we left Tetbury.'

'Ten o'clock! It was eleven, upon my soul! I counted every stroke! Ha! This brother of yours would persuade me out of my senses, Miss Morland! Just look at my horse! Did you ever see an animal so made for speed in your life?'

Catherine looked at the horse. 'He *does* look rather hot, to be sure,' she said, doubtfully.

'Hot! He is as fresh as the moment we left! What d'you think of my carriage, Miss Morland? A neat one, is it not? What d'you think I gave for it? Hey?'

'I am sure I have no idea.'

'Fifty pounds!' Catherine did not know whether this was cheap or dear, so she said nothing. 'Are you fond of an open carriage, Miss Morland?'

'Oh yes, very.' Catherine was pleased to be asked a question on which she had an opinion. 'But I have hardly ever had an opportunity of being in one.'

'I am glad of it,' said John. 'I will drive you out in mine every day!'

'Thank you,' said Catherine, in some distress. There was a few moments' silence. Then, timidly: 'Have you ever read *Udolpho*, Mr Thorpe?'

'*Udolpho*!' he cried. 'Lord, no, I never read novels! I have better things to do with my time!'

Catherine was rather glad when they all moved off together to call on Mrs Thorpe. Although she was not entirely pleased by John's manners, she told herself that he was her brother's dear friend and her dear friend's brother, so he could not be entirely without merit. And when Isabella afterwards assured her that John thought her the most charming girl in the world and he had engaged her to dance with him that night at the ball, she decided he was quite an agreeable gentleman after all.

Although she would, of course, have much preferred to dance with Mr Tilney.

Chapter 5
The Second Ball

'My dear creature,' said Isabella, 'I am afraid I must leave you. Your brother is so amazingly impatient to dance!'

Mr and Mrs Allen and Catherine had arrived at the Upper Rooms to find the Thorpes already there. Isabella went through the usual smiling ritual on meeting her friend, admiring her gown and the curl of her hair, before taking to the dance floor with James. Catherine had, of course, been engaged to dance with John, but he was nowhere to be seen, so she was left without a partner once more, sitting between the two older ladies while the others danced.

She was roused from this state of humiliation by seeing, not Mr Thorpe, but … Mr Tilney! He was making his way through the crowds, looking as handsome as ever and talking in a lively way to a pleasant-looking young woman who was leaning on his arm. This was clearly his sister, Catherine decided. Mr Tilney had never mentioned that he had a wife, or a beloved, so how could it possibly be anyone else?

Our heroine watched, sitting perfectly erect, her cheeks only a little redder than usual, as Mr Tilney and his companion continued their approach through the crowd. They were with an older lady, who stopped to speak to Mrs Thorpe, and this time Catherine succeeded in catching Mr Tilney's eye. She instantly received a smile of recognition, which she returned with pleasure.

Mrs Allen greeted him warmly as he came over. 'I am very happy to see you again, sir, indeed. Catherine and I were terribly afraid that you had left Bath for good, were we not, Catherine?'

Catherine felt her cheeks grow even redder than before.

Mr Tilney bowed. 'I was called away for a few days, madam, on the very morning after we met.'

'And now you are returned!' said Mrs Allen. 'And we are so very pleased to see you, are we not, Catherine? I was only saying just now, what a shame it is that our dear Catherine finds herself without a dance partner once again, was I not, Catherine?'

'It is indeed a pity, madam. But perhaps we can rectify the situation. Miss Morland?'

He held out his hand, but before Catherine could take it, a loud voice came from behind: 'Hey-dey, Miss Morland! What is the meaning of this? I thought you and I were to dance together!'

It was John Thorpe. If he had not been the brother of her dear friend Isabella, Catherine would have wished him anywhere else in the world. But he was, and she had no choice. She had promised to dance with him, so dance with him she must.

'What chap have you there, Miss Morland?' he said as they went over to the dance floor. 'Hey?'

Miss Morland satisfied his curiosity.

'Tilney,' he repeated. 'Tilney. I know a *General* Tilney, fine old fellow, famously rich, I should like to dine with him. But that one, no, I do not know him. Does he want a horse?'

Miss Morland replied that she did not know.

'Friend of mine, Sam Fletcher, has got one to sell, famous clever animal, only forty pounds. I would buy it myself, but it would not suit my purpose. I would give any money for a real good hunter, of course. I have three now, best in the county, anybody will tell you, I would not take eight hundred pounds for them. Are you fond of horses, Miss Morland?'

Miss Morland said she had very little experience of them, but certainly admired those she knew.

There was a short pause in which John stepped on the hem of her gown and she pretended not to notice. Then: 'Old Allen is rich as a king, is he not?' he said suddenly.

Catherine did not at first understand.

'Old Allen,' John repeated, impatiently. 'The man you are with.'

'Oh! Mr Allen, you mean. Yes, I believe he is quite wealthy.'

'And you are his favourite, hey? You are always with him.'

'Well, yes, but—'

'Ha! Well, he seems a good enough old fellow and quite getting on in years. Does he want a horse?'

Catherine was glad when the dance was over and she was able to plead tiredness and return to her place beside Mrs Allen and her friend.

'Well, my dear,' said Mrs Thorpe. 'I hope you had an agreeable partner. Dear John has charming manners, does he not?'

Mrs Allen saved Catherine from the need to reply to this difficult question. 'Did you meet Mr Tilney, my dear?' she said.

'No – where is he, Mrs Allen? Did you see where he went?'

'He was with us just now, dear, but then said he was tired of sitting and resolved to go and dance. I thought he might be looking for you.'

Catherine looked around at the sea of people, but was unable to see him.

'Oh! There he is! Leading a young lady to the dance!' Mrs Allen peered across the room. 'What an odd-looking creature. Do we know her, Mrs Thorpe? Strange gown.' She patted Catherine's hand. 'I do wish he had found you, dear,' she said. 'He is such an agreeable young man.'

Catherine sighed and was wondering how to reply when she was interrupted by a voice:

'Miss Morland? I think you might know my brother?'

It was the young lady who had arrived with Mr Tilney. Although not as fashionable as Isabella, she had a charming face and an air of true elegance – and she was (as Catherine had suspected) Mr Tilney's younger sister. Our heroine was quite sure they would be friends.

'How well your brother dances, Miss Tilney!' said Catherine, after they had been chatting for a few minutes.

'Henry?'

Henry! So that was his first name!

Miss Tilney was looking over at the dance floor. 'Yes, he does dance well.'

'And the young lady he is dancing with? Is she someone you know?'

'A Miss Smith, I believe. She is an acquaintance of our aunt.'

'Oh! Well, I dare say she is glad to have a partner.' Catherine watched the young lady for a moment. Then: 'Do you think her pretty, Miss Tilney?'

Miss Tilney smiled. 'Not very,' she said. 'I believe Henry might be dancing with her out of kindness.'

Catherine smiled back at her, now perfectly sure they would be friends.

* * *

'At last I have got you!' Catherine found her arm seized by her faithful Isabella. 'My dearest creature, I have been looking for you everywhere! Why did you not come and find me?'

'My dear Isabella, how was that possible? I could not even see where you were!'

'That is what I told your brother, but he would not believe me! "Go and find her, Mr Morland," I said. "Go and find your sister!" But he would not shift one inch. Oh, these men, Catherine! He was determined to have the next dance with me, and the next, and there was no arguing with him!'

Catherine drew her away a short distance. 'Look at that young lady with the white beads round her head,' she whispered. 'It is Mr Tilney's sister!'

'Oh! Goodness! You don't say so! What a delightful girl! But where is the famous brother? Point him out to me this instant, I die to see him! Oh! And who is the older gentleman who keeps looking over this way? Is it you he is looking at? Or me?'

It was not until the end of the evening that Catherine found out.

* * *

'That gentleman is General Tilney, my father. He has been asking about you, Miss Morland.'

Catherine had been searching for Mr Tilney, but instead had found his sister coming out of the supper room.

'About me? Why would he ask about me?'

Miss Tilney smiled. 'Perhaps because he has seen you with my brother.'

'Oh!' Catherine felt her cheeks grow hot and found herself unable to speak, so Miss Tilney continued. 'Have you taken a country walk since you arrived in Bath, Miss Morland?'

Miss Morland said she hadn't.

'That is indeed a pity,' replied her new friend. 'There is little my brother and I enjoy more. The countryside around Bath is so delightful, we go out together most days. Perhaps you would like to join us, some day or other?'

'Oh!' Catherine's eyes sparkled as she looked at her new friend. 'Dear Miss Tilney, I should like that more than anything in the world!'

'Good,' said Miss Tilney. 'That is settled then. Perhaps one day next week … ?'

'No, no, no! Do not let us put it off! Let us go tomorrow!'

Miss Tilney smiled. 'Very well,' she said. 'Henry and I will call for you at twelve o'clock. So long as it does not rain, of course.'

Catherine was quite sure it would not rain. And: 'Remember! Twelve o'clock!' was her parting call to her new friend before she got into the carriage with Mr and Mrs Allen and danced in her seat all the way home.

Chapter 6
Disaster!

It was raining. No matter how many times Catherine looked out of the window the next morning, or how many times she checked with Mrs Allen, there was no denying it: the sun did not shine; the day was wet. It was raining.

'Perhaps it will come to nothing,' she said for the twentieth time. 'It may clear up before twelve.'

'It may, my dear,' said Mrs Allen. 'But then, you know, it will be so muddy. You will have to be careful of your gown.'

'Oh! That will not matter!' said Catherine. 'I never mind mud!'

'No,' replied the older lady, placidly. 'I know you never mind mud.'

Catherine looked out of the window again. 'Oh, Mrs Allen! It comes on faster and faster! There are umbrellas up already. How I hate the sight of an umbrella!'

'They are very disagreeable things to carry, to be sure,' said Mrs Allen. 'There will be few people at the Pump Room if it rains all the morning. I hope Mr Allen will put on his coat when he goes out, but I dare say he will not.'

Catherine went every five minutes to look at the clock, telling herself each time that if it kept raining another five minutes she would give up the matter as hopeless. But the clock struck twelve and still it rained.

'You will not be able to go, my dear,' said Mrs Allen. 'I am afraid Miss Tilney and her brother will not come.'

'I shall give it till a quarter past twelve.'

Catherine gave it till a quarter past twelve, then twenty past, then twenty-five. Finally, at half past twelve, the sky did begin to clear and a gleam of sunshine broke through the clouds. But had there been too much rain for Miss Tilney and her brother to venture out? Were the streets too muddy for their walk?

She had almost given up hope when there was a loud rap on the door.

'Make haste, make haste!' a voice called up the stairs. 'Put on your hat this moment, Miss Morland! We are going to Bristol!'

It was John Thorpe. Catherine looked out of the window to see two carriages stopped outside the house.

'Bristol?' said Catherine, as John Thorpe entered the room. 'Is that not a great way off?'

'My sweetest Catherine!' Isabella was followed, as usual, by Catherine's brother James. 'Is not this delightful? We shall have the most glorious drive!'

'But I cannot come with you,' said Catherine. 'I expect

some friends any moment. We are going for a country walk.'

'Friends?' said John Thorpe. 'What friends?'

'Miss Tilney and her brother. They promised to come at twelve, only it was raining. But now it is fine, I am sure they will be here soon.'

'Tilney?' said John. 'Is that the chap I saw you with last night? Ha! He will not come!'

'What? How do you know that, Mr Thorpe?'

'Because I saw him, just now as we turned into Broad Street. Driving in a carriage with a very smart-looking girl. Heading out of the city.'

'How odd,' said Catherine. 'Are you sure it was him?'

'Oh yes, yes, yes, quite sure. I knew him directly.'

'Oh ... I suppose he thought there was too much mud for a walk.'

'And well he might! I never saw so much mud in my life. Walk!' John gave a short laugh. 'You could no more walk than you could fly.'

'But what if they come back, now the weather is dry? They may come back, you know.'

'No danger of that!' said John Thorpe. 'I heard him call out to a man who was passing on horseback, did I not, Morland?' James shrugged his shoulders, so John continued. 'He said they were going as far as Wick Rock, far beyond the boundaries of the city. Ha!

I fear he has quite forgotten your arrangement, Miss Morland.'

Isabella took Catherine's arm. 'My dearest, sweetest creature, you cannot refuse now. You must come with us.'

'Oh, I do not know. Shall I go, Mrs Allen?'

'Just as you please, my dear.'

'Mrs Allen, you must persuade her!' was the general cry. 'We cannot go without her! It will quite spoil our drive!'

'Well, my dear,' Mrs Allen said, 'in that case I suppose you should.'

So it was decided, and in two minutes they were off.

Catherine's feelings as she got in the carriage with John Thorpe (Isabella rode in the other with James) were very confused. She was hurt that the Tilneys seemed to think so little of her that they gave up their engagement without sending any message or excuse, and she did not think they had behaved well. On the other hand, she was determined to enjoy the carriage ride. Even if it was with John Thorpe.

* * *

They had been driving for a short while when Catherine was roused by some words from her companion: 'Who is that girl who looked at you so hard as we went by?'

'What girl?' said Catherine. 'Where?'

'On the right-hand pavement.'

Catherine look round and saw Miss Tilney, leaning on her brother's arm.

'Stop!' she cried. 'Mr Thorpe, stop! It is Miss Tilney!'

Miss Tilney and her brother had stopped and were both looking back at her as the carriage drove past.

'Stop!' she cried again. 'I must get out and speak to them!'

It was no good. John Thorpe only lashed his horse to a brisker trot and the Tilneys were soon out of sight.

'Please, Mr Thorpe!' cried Catherine. 'Please stop! I must go back to Miss Tilney!'

But John just laughed and encouraged his horse to go faster. Catherine felt her cheeks grow hot with anger and her eyes prickle with tears.

'How could you deceive me, Mr Thorpe?' she said. 'How could you say you saw them driving out of the city?'

John shrugged. 'Thought it was him,' he said. 'Never saw two men look so alike in my life.'

'They will think it so strange, so rude of me. Oh, Mr Thorpe, how could you?'

The drive had not begun well and it got no better. Catherine was too angry and pained to speak, so they went on in silence. They had been driving for an hour or so, when there was a shout from James in the carriage behind.

'We had better go back, John,' he said when his friend had stopped. 'It is too late to go on today. We did not set out in enough time to get to Bristol and back by nightfall. We had much better turn around and put it off to another day.'

'It is all one to me,' said John angrily. He turned his horse around and they were soon on their way back to Bath.

When they finally arrived and Catherine entered the house, her worst fears were realized. A gentleman and a lady had called for her, the footman said, just a few minutes after she had left, and had seemed surprised when he told them she had gone out with Mr Thorpe. So the Tilneys had come after all!

It was with a heavy heart that Catherine went to bed that night, and by the time she fell asleep, long after the house had fallen silent, her pillow was wet with tears.

What must the Tilneys think of her? How could she ever explain?

Chapter 7
Joy!

'Do not forget, my dear,' said Mrs Allen, 'we are engaged to go to the theatre this evening.'

Catherine had woken up feeling just as miserable as the night before. But she could think of no good excuse for staying at home, so to the theatre she went. It was a play she had very much wanted to see, a comedy, and in spite of her troubles, she succeeded in enjoying the first part so much that no one would have guessed she had cried herself to sleep the night before.

Then came the interval. And she saw him. Mr Tilney and his father had joined a group of people in the box at the other side of the theatre. Had he seen her? And what would she do if he had?

Our poor heroine found herself completely unable to enjoy the next part of the play. She could not concentrate on the stage at all, but just watched Henry Tilney in the opposite box, not knowing whether to hope or fear that she would catch his eye.

And then the play was over. The curtain had fallen and the audience had started to leave when she saw him, making his way through the rows of seats towards them. Catherine did not wait for him to speak. She had too much to say herself.

'Oh Mr Tilney!' she cried. 'I have been quite wild to speak to you and make my apologies! You must have thought me so rude! And Miss Tilney! But indeed, it was not my fault – was it, Mrs Allen? My friend's brother told me, did he not, that he had seen Mr Tilney and his sister going out in a carriage together! And then, what could I do? They begged me so hard to go with them! But I had ten thousand times rather have been with you – had I not, Mrs Allen?'

'My dear, you rumple my gown,' was that lady's reply.

'I begged Mr Thorpe to stop!' continued Catherine. 'I called out to him the moment I saw you, did I not, Mrs Allen? Oh, you were not there! But I did, Mr Tilney! And if Mr Thorpe would only have stopped, I would have jumped out and run after you as fast as I could! Would I not, Mrs Allen?'

Is there a Henry in the world who could be unmoved by such a declaration? If so, it was not Henry Tilney. He smiled, he bowed, he reassured our heroine that neither he nor his sister were angry or shocked by her behaviour. They had known that some unexpected event must have occurred to prevent Catherine from keeping their appointment and then – oh, joy! – the country walk was arranged for the very next day!

* * *

Catherine left the theatre one of the happiest creatures in the world and woke the next morning to sunshine streaming through her window. The Tilneys called for her at the appointed time and Miss Tilney greeted her with smiles and kindness. It was as if the events of the previous day had never happened and so, with a light heart and a spring in her step, our heroine set off with her friends.

'I never look at a river,' said Catherine, 'without thinking of the south of France.'

They were walking alongside the river as far as Beechen Cliff, a beauty spot that was much admired by every visitor to Bath.

Mr Tilney looked at her, surprised. 'You have been abroad, Miss Morland?'

'Oh no! I only meant what I have read about it! The sight of a river always puts me in mind of the country where Emily travelled in *Udolpho*! That was the south of France, was it not? Or was it Italy? Spain? Oh! These countries are all so very much alike, are they not?' She looked at Mr Tilney. 'But I dare say you never read novels, do you?'

'Why not?'

'Because they are not clever enough for you. I thought gentlemen read better books, full of facts and dates and numbers, things of that sort.'

'The person,' said Mr Tilney, 'be it a gentleman or a lady, who does not enjoy a good novel must be intolerably stupid. Once I began *Udolpho*, I could not put it down. I finished it in two days – my hair standing on end the whole time.'

'Yes,' added Miss Tilney, 'and then you decided to read it aloud to me – and I also enjoyed it immensely.'

Catherine could not hide her delight. 'I am so very glad to hear it,' she said. 'If you like novels I shall never be ashamed of liking them again!'

'You are fond of that kind of reading?' said Miss Tilney.

'To tell you the truth, I do not much like any other. I can read poetry and plays and things of that sort. But history, real serious history, I cannot be interested in. Can you, Miss Tilney?'

'Yes, I admit I am fond of history.'

'I wish I were, but it tells me nothing that interests me. The quarrels of kings, with wars and troubles every day – and hardly any women or girls! It is very tiresome. I sometimes think history was just invented by men to torture little children.'

Mr Tilney tried not to smile and the walk continued in the same delightful way.

* * *

Although the walk ended too soon, it ended as happily as it had begun. Catherine's friends accompanied her to her door and arrangements were made for the three of them to meet at the ball the following night. Our heroine could barely hide her pleasure at such a delightful prospect.

This pleasure turned to surprise when she found Isabella waiting for her in the house, wearing a look of happy importance.

'Oh, my dearest Catherine, where have you been? I have been waiting this past hour! But I see you have already guessed my news!'

'Indeed I have not.'

'Nay, my beloved, sweetest friend, you know your Isabella's heart better than she does herself.'

'Believe me, Isabella, I do not.'

'Sly creature! You are so like your dear brother, I quite doted on you the moment I saw you. But so it always is with me – that first moment settles everything. The very first day your brother came to us last Christmas – I was wearing my yellow gown, I remember, with my hair done up in braids – I thought I never saw anyone so handsome in my life.'

Catherine was very fond of her brother but she had never thought him handsome. She looked at Isabella and the truth darted into her mind. 'My dear Isabella! Do you mean – can you really be – in love with James?'

'Oh my dearest, sweetest Catherine, you have guessed my secret! It is true! Your brother has made me the happiest woman in the world! We are soon to be more than friends, my Catherine. We are to be sisters!'

'My dear Isabella, you cannot mean – ?'

'Yes! Your brother and I are engaged to be married.'

Chapter 8
The Third Ball

'A famous good thing, this marrying scheme, hey? What d'you say, Miss Morland?'

The Tilneys had not yet arrived, so our heroine was obliged to talk to Isabella's brother. Catherine's own brother had gone back to the family home at Fullerton to give their parents the happy news, and to discuss a marriage settlement with his father, so Isabella was without a partner, and was obliged to sit with the older ladies at the side of the room.

'I am sure you are right, Mr Thorpe,' said Catherine. 'I am very happy for Isabella and my brother.'

'Are you indeed?' John Thorpe's face seemed even redder than usual. 'I am very glad to hear it, very glad indeed!'

Catherine said nothing. She had just seen Mr and Miss Tilney enter the room, accompanied by a very handsome and fashionable-looking young man. This must be their brother, the famous Captain Tilney that they had told her about. She looked at him with great admiration, and even supposed it possible that some people might think him more handsome than his brother. She, however, found his looks and his manner decidedly inferior. He had not got any of Henry's sweetness or his quiet charm, his fine dark eyes, his—

'Did you ever hear that old saying, Miss Morland?' John's voice interrupted her thoughts. '"Going to one wedding brings on another"?'

Miss Morland did not think she had.

'Ah! You will come to Isabella's wedding, I presume?' said John.

'What? Oh, yes.' Catherine was watching Henry Tilney as he made his way through the crowds, talking to his sister who was laughing at something he had said. 'I have promised her I will be there, certainly.'

'And then, you never know ... ' John gave a strange forced laugh and fidgeted with his collar. 'You never know ... we – you and I, I mean ... may test out the truth of that old saying! What d'you say to that, Miss Morland? Hey?'

Miss Morland had no idea what he was talking about. 'May we? Yes, I suppose so. Excuse me, Mr Thorpe, but I have just seen my friends and I must go to them.'

'Nay, there is no need to hurry off, Miss Morland!' He tried to block her way. 'Who knows when we may be together again? I shall be leaving Bath tomorrow for a week, and a very long week it will seem.'

'Then why stay away so long?' said Catherine vaguely, trying to edge away.

'That is kind of you, Miss Morland, very kind.' He ran a finger round the back of his collar and suddenly burst out: 'I do not know anybody like you, Miss Morland!'

'Really? I dare say there are a great many people like me, only a good deal better, Mr Thorpe. Excuse me, I really must go to my friends.'

And away our heroine went, leaving us feeling only a little sorry for John Thorpe.

* * *

'That gentleman would have put me out of patience if he had kept you a moment longer,' said Mr Tilney, after the usual pleasantries had been exchanged. 'He has no business keeping my dance partner from me.'

'Mr Thorpe is such a very particular friend of my brother,' said Catherine, 'that if he talks to me, I must talk to him.'

Before Mr Tilney could reply, they were interrupted by Captain Tilney, who, much to Catherine's dissatisfaction, pulled his brother away. They retired whispering together for a full five minutes, during which time Catherine was in an agony of suspense. Had Captain Tilney heard something about her, which he was now communicating to his brother in the hope of separating them forever? She felt she was about to die of apprehension when Henry finally returned and asked her if she thought her friend Miss Thorpe would have any objection to dancing. His brother had asked to be introduced to her.

'Oh, no!' said Catherine. 'I am quite sure that Isabella does not mean to dance at all.' Her friend was engaged to James, after all – she would never dance with another man!

'Hmm.' Mr Tilney was looking across the room towards the dance floor. 'I fear Miss Thorpe takes a somewhat different view.'

Catherine was astonished to see Captain Tilney leading Isabella into the dance.

'Oh!' she cried. 'I am sure ... your brother probably saw Isabella on her own, and supposed she might wish for a partner. It is very good-natured of him, I am sure. He could not know that she is engaged to my brother.'

'Dear Miss Morland,' said Mr Tilney, 'it is a sign of your superior nature that you view my brother's behaviour as an act of kindness.'

'I do not understand you.'

Mr Tilney smiled. 'Then we are on very unequal terms, Miss Morland, for I understand you very well.'

Catherine was still unsure of his meaning, but he looked at her with such sweetness in his eyes that she did not mind.

* * *

It was not until later that our heroine had the opportunity to question her friend. How could she, an engaged woman, dance with another man?

'Oh! I do not wonder at your surprise,' said Isabella. 'I did not want to dance with the conceited fellow! I would much rather sit still.'

'Then why did you?'

'I refused him as long as I could, but he would not take no for an answer. Such nonsense! I begged him to excuse me, to find another partner, but no! There was nobody else in the room he could bear to think of as a partner, and it was not just that he wanted to dance with me, he wanted to *be* with me! I saw there would be no peace if I did not agree to just one dance. And then, of course, since he is such a smart young fellow, I saw every eye upon us, so I could not refuse to dance with him again.'

'He is a very handsome young man.'

'Is he? Well, I suppose some people might say so, but his looks are not to my taste. But let us not talk of him, dearest Catherine. Let us talk about your dear brother. Have you had word from him? Has he spoken to your father yet about our marriage?'

Before Catherine could reply, they were interrupted by the arrival of Miss Tilney.

'I beg your pardon, Miss Morland,' she said. 'But my

father has asked me to speak to you.'

'Your father!' Catherine looked over to see General Tilney deep in conversation with John Thorpe. Her cheeks grew hot as she saw them look in her direction. Were they talking about her? If so, what could they be saying?

'Yes,' continued Miss Tilney. 'He has decided that we must all leave Bath within the next few days and return to our home in the country.'

'In the next few days! Oh, Miss Tilney!' Then: 'And Mr Tilney? Will he be leaving too?'

The prospect of a Bath with no Henry Tilney in it was indeed a miserable one.

'Yes. My father has been disappointed by some friends and is in a hurry to get home.'

'I am very sorry for it,' said Catherine.

'And that is why my father—'

'Well, Eleanor!' came a voice from behind. 'Have you asked her?' It was General Tilney. Catherine saw her friend's face flush. There was something about her father's presence that seemed to make her uncomfortable.

'I was just beginning to, sir,' said Eleanor, her voice faltering as she spoke. 'But—'

'My daughter has a request to make, Miss Morland,' he said, interrupting her again. 'She has told you we plan to leave Bath in the next few days? Well! You would make your friend very happy if you would oblige her with your company.'

Catherine could not believe her ears. Did he mean ... ?

'We can offer you none of the amusements of this lively place,' the General continued, 'but we will try to make your stay at Northanger Abbey as pleasant as possible, will we not, Eleanor?'

Northanger Abbey! Our heroine was unable to speak. Her passion for ancient buildings was almost equal to her passion for Henry Tilney – and now she was to experience both! She was invited to stay in a real abbey, just like the ones she had read about, full of secrets and shadows and ghostly happenings – and with Henry Tilney in it!

'Dear Miss Morland,' Eleanor said in a low voice as she squeezed Catherine's hand, 'please say yes. It would make me so happy if you could come.'

'I will write home directly!' said Catherine. 'But I am sure my parents will agree!'

And so it was settled. Our heroine was going to Northanger Abbey. Her happiness was complete.

Part 2

60

Chapter 1
The Journey

'It seems you have formed a very favourable idea of the Abbey, Miss Morland. I hope you will not be disappointed.'

The journey had begun. Catherine found herself with Mr Tilney in his open carriage, as happy a being as ever existed. Her companion drove so well, without lashing his horse or shouting or explaining to her what a very good driver he was – it was all very different to the last ride she had taken, with a certain other gentleman. And then, Mr Tilney's hat suited him so well, and his fine coat made him look so delightfully important! To be driven by him, next to dancing with him, was the greatest happiness in the world.

'Is it not a grand old place?' said Catherine. 'Just like those one reads about in books?'

Mr Tilney smiled. 'Of course! But are you prepared for the horrors that such an ancient building may contain, Miss Morland? Are you brave enough to face the secret passages and gloomy staircases and bloodstained flagstones?'

'Oh, I do not think I shall be easily frightened,' said Catherine. 'There will be other people there, will there not? I will not be left on my own with only a flickering candle to light my way, as generally happens in such places.'

'That is true,' said Mr Tilney. 'But you must know that when a young lady comes to stay in a building of this kind, she is always given a room far away from the rest of the family. While they retire to their own part of the house, she is led by Dorothy, the ancient one-eyed housekeeper, up a different staircase and along many gloomy passages to a room that has not been used since some long-lost ancestor died there over one hundred years ago.'

'Oh! But this will not happen to me, I am sure.' Catherine looked at him. 'Will it?'

'Dorothy then shows you into your room, a great shadowy chamber with tapestries covering the walls and an ancient four-poster bed hung with drapes of dark green and purple velvet.'

'Oh! Mr Tilney! How frightful! This is just like a book! What happens next?'

'How fearfully you will examine your room, Miss Morland, by the feeble light of your single lamp. What do you see? There is no chair, no desk, no comfortable place to sit. On one side there is an ancient chest containing who knows what, and on the other, the portrait of a handsome lord, whose sad eyes seem to watch you from his place high up above the fireplace.'

'Is he the ancestor who died there, Mr Tilney? In my room?'

'You do not know.' He looked at her from the corner of his eye. 'And then, after Dorothy has told you—'

'Oh, is Dorothy still there? I thought she had gone.'

'No, she is still there. She has some important information to impart.'

'Oh, I see. Go on.'

'She tells you that this wing of the Abbey is definitely haunted and that there will be no one close enough to hear you call out in the night. Only then does she leave you alone.'

'Ah, of course! What next?'

'You listen to the sound of her footsteps as they fade away down the corridor and then ... *silence*!'

'Ooh!'

'You rush to your door and discover, with increasing alarm, that it has no lock!'

'Oh, Mr Tilney, this is frightful! But it cannot happen to me. I am sure your housekeeper is not really called Dorothy. Go on.'

'That night,' said Mr Tilney, 'you are woken by a violent storm. Peals of thunder so loud they seem to shake the old building to its foundations, a gust of wind that nearly extinguishes your lamp—'

'Oh, have I left the lamp burning? That was wise.'

'In its feeble light you can just make out one part of the wall-hanging that is moving more violently in the wind than the rest. Unable to repress your curiosity, you get up and find a break in the tapestry – behind it, a hidden door which, after a few efforts, you succeed in opening, and, with your lamp in your hand, you pass through and find yourself in a small vaulted room.'

'No, indeed. I should be much too frightened to do any such thing. Go on.'

'At one side of this room is a large old-fashioned cabinet, made of gold and ebony, towards which you feel irresistibly drawn. You unlock its doors, go through every drawer, searching, searching, searching for you know not what – '

'Oh! Oh, and do I find it?'

'Not at first. Until ... '

'Yes?'

'At last, you touch a hidden spring and a secret compartment opens. You feel inside and your fingers touch ... a roll of paper – '

'A mysterious document! Signed in blood, I suspect! What is written on it, Mr Tilney?'

'You seize it, you hasten back to your own room, but scarcely have you started to unroll the paper when ... your lamp goes out, leaving you in total darkness.'

'No, no, no, do not say so!' Catherine found she was clutching the hem of her jacket very tightly with both hands. 'Well?' She looked at Mr Tilney. 'What happens then?'

But Mr Tilney was laughing far too much to carry on and Catherine, having become a little embarrassed by her own excitement, assured him most earnestly that she wasn't in the least concerned that her stay at Northanger Abbey would be anything like the one he described.

'Miss Tilney, I am sure, would never put me in a room like that,' she said, adding that she was really not in the least afraid.

As they drew near the end of the journey, Catherine became increasingly impatient for a sight of the Abbey. At every bend in the road, she expected to have a glimpse of its grey stone walls and ancient battlements, the last rays of the evening sun reflecting on its Gothic windows. But it was getting dark as they grew close, and they were actually through the gates and outside the main door before she knew it.

Our heroine had arrived!

Chapter 2
The First Night

A moment's glance was enough to satisfy Catherine that her room was completely unlike the one that Mr Tilney had described. It was neither particularly large nor horribly gloomy and it contained no tapestries nor anything at all made of purple velvet. The walls were papered, the floor carpeted and the furniture was handsome and comfortable. There was nothing to be afraid of here!

She had just finished getting changed for dinner when there was a knock at the door. It was Miss Tilney, come to see if she was ready. Her father, she said, was very particular about meals being served on time, and it was already getting late.

Miss Tilney's fears were not altogether unfounded, for when she and Catherine ran down the stairs together they found General Tilney pacing the hallway with his watch in his hand. As soon as they appeared he rang the bell for the servants (Catherine had never seen so many servants in one house before) and shouted an order: 'Dinner to be on the table *now*!'

Catherine was rather shocked at the violence of his request. She had noticed that both the General's younger children were always rather subdued in his presence, that Henry's lively cheerfulness and Eleanor's smiling sweetness were not particularly evident when their father was around, but she found him a charming and distinguished gentleman. He seemed so very interested in *her*, asking about her family, where they lived, what their house was like, and about her relationship with Mr and Mrs Allen whom, like John Thorpe, he seemed to believe were extremely wealthy.

'I suppose, Miss Morland,' he said, as they sat down at the table, 'that you are used to a much larger dining room than this when you dine at the Allens'?'

'Oh! No, indeed!' said Catherine. 'Mr Allen's dining room is not more than half the size and nowhere near as noble and luxurious! In fact, I do not believe that I have ever been in a room as large as this in my entire life!'

General Tilney seemed pleased and his good humour increased as the meal went on, but it was not until he finally excused himself and left the young people alone that Catherine's friends became themselves again. The rest of the evening passed pleasantly, but our heroine was tired after her journey and was not sorry when it was time to go to bed.

The night was a stormy one; the wind had been rising steadily since they arrived, and by the time the friends said goodnight, it blew and rained violently. As Catherine crossed the hall, she listened to the storm as it raged around the ancient building and closed with sudden fury a distant door, and she felt for the first time that she really was in an abbey. The sounds reminded her of so many horrid scenes in the books she'd read that she was glad to reach her own snug room and remind herself that Miss Tilney was sleeping only two doors away. Mr Tilney had certainly been joking when he described her visit in such terrifying terms – *she* had nothing to fear from sinister housekeepers and secret doors!

How glad I am, she thought, *that Northanger Abbey is nothing like those places one reads about in books!*

She looked around the room and, by the light of her flickering candle, saw that the curtains at the windows seemed to be moving. It was nothing but the wind, of course, she told herself as she got ready for bed.

And then she saw it.

An old-fashioned cabinet, set back in a recess at the side of the fireplace. How could Catherine have failed to notice it before? She picked up her candle, and stepped closer to examine it. It was a large piece of furniture, clearly very old, and made of gold and ebony, just like the one Mr Tilney had described. It was nothing more than a coincidence, of course, but Catherine was intrigued. The key was in the door of the cabinet, so she decided to look inside – not with the smallest expectation of finding anything of course, just that it was so very odd, after what Mr Tilney had said. So, placing her candle carefully on a nearby chair, our heroine seized the key with one trembling hand and tried to turn it. It moved a little and she believed herself successful, but – how strangely mysterious! – the door still would not open.

Catherine paused a moment in breathless wonder. The wind roared down the chimney, the rain beat in torrents against the windows, but she was determined she would not give up. She tried the key again and after moving it in every possible way the door of the cabinet suddenly sprang open. Catherine's heart leapt. Inside was a double range of small drawers with some larger drawers above and below and, in the centre, a small compartment, also closed with a lock and key. *This,* thought Catherine, *was almost certainly where any treasure or secret documents would be concealed.* But she would search the drawers first.

Our heroine's heart beat fast, but her courage did not fail her. With cheeks flushed with hope and eyes straining with curiosity, her fingers grasped the handle of a drawer and pulled it open. It was empty. She seized a second, a third, a fourth – each was equally empty. Not one was left unsearched and in not one was anything found. The place in the middle was now the only part left unexplored.

It would be foolish not to examine every part of the cabinet, Catherine told herself, although she knew there was almost certainly no chance of finding anything. But if there *was* anything to be found it was bound to be in there, in that central compartment.

It was some time before she could unlock the doors, but at length they did open and, by the light of her flickering candle, she saw that her search had not been in vain. There was something there! A roll of paper that had been pushed right to the back of the cavity – just as if someone had wanted to hide it. Catherine's heart fluttered, her knees trembled, and, with a shaking hand, she reached inside and withdrew the precious manuscript.

A sudden dimming in the light of her candle made her turn in alarm, but there was no danger – it had some hours left to burn. But then, just as she was about to unroll the mysterious manuscript and discover its secrets, a sudden gust of wind blew out the candle, plunging the room into darkness. For a few moments, Catherine was motionless with fear. Blackness, impenetrable and solid, filled the room. The violence of the wind, rising with sudden fury, added to the horror of the moment.

Catherine trembled from head to foot, a cold sweat stood out on her forehead and the manuscript fell from her hand. She groped her way over to the bed and jumped in, hiding her head under the covers. But this did not stop her hearing, in the silence that followed, the sound of footsteps in the corridor outside her door ...

Chapter 3
The Mysterious Door

'I hope you were not too much disturbed by the storm, Miss Morland?'

Catherine had come down to breakfast the next morning to find Mr Tilney sitting alone at the table reading a book.

'Oh ... the wind did keep me awake a little,' she said. 'But I would not say I was *disturbed*, no, not *disturbed*.'

'In spite of me scaring you with my silly stories?'

'Certainly not! I did not give them a second thought! Oh, look! What beautiful hyacinths!'

Catherine was not going to confess to Mr Tilney what had really happened: how she had lain awake for hours listening to the storm and imagining all sorts of noises in the corridor outside her room. And then, when she had woken the next morning to sunshine streaming through the curtains, she had instantly remembered the mysterious document she had dropped in the darkness and sprung out of bed to collect the scattered sheets from the floor. How her greedy eye had glanced rapidly over the first page and – no! It could not be true! What she saw was not some ancient and interesting document – not a tear-stained love letter written to a long-lost sweetheart or a ghastly confession signed in blood – but a new-looking sheet of paper covered in neat, modern handwriting …

'Socks,' she had read, 'three pairs. Stockings, six pairs. Three waistcoats, two cravats, one petticoat … '

It was a modern-day laundry list!

Two other sheets, written by the same hand, listed expenses that were scarcely more interesting: envelopes, hair-powder, string, soap. A shopping list! Such was the collection of papers (left behind by some careless servant, she guessed) that had filled her with such excitement and robbed her of her night's rest.

So, no. Catherine was not going to tell that to Mr Tilney, even though he was looking at her with an amused smile on his lips and a twinkle in his eye.

She was saved from the embarrassment of further questions by the arrival of General Tilney and his daughter. The General proposed they would spend the morning showing Miss Morland around the Abbey and its grounds. Miss Morland had rather hoped to explore accompanied only by his son and daughter, but Henry had to pay a visit to Woodston, a nearby village where he ran a small farm, and the General was most insistent: he would show her round himself or not at all!

And so it was that the three of them set out after breakfast. Catherine had been impatient to see the house and was at first struck by its grandeur and impressed by the beauty of its grounds. But after they had viewed the kitchen garden, the orchard and a succession of hothouses, and the General had described the large variety of fruits and vegetables he grew there and his preferred methods of cultivation, she found herself becoming a little weary of him and his questions: 'Were Mr Allen's grounds as extensive as these?' he wanted to know. 'What about his orchard?' And he supposed that 'Mr Allen has a great many fine hothouses in which he raises fruit and vegetables for the table?'

Catherine answered that Mr Allen's grounds were not at all extensive, he had no orchard and only one rather small hothouse where Mrs Allen kept her plants in the winter.

The General appeared pleased with this information and, with a triumphant smile of self-satisfaction, continued his tour. When he suggested that the girls might like to view some alterations he was planning to one of the outhouses, Miss Tilney finally spoke up: perhaps Miss Morland would like to see another part of the grounds? There was a favourite walk of hers that she would very much like Miss Morland to see.

'What?' said the General. 'Why would you take her on that cold, damp path? Miss Morland does not want to go that way! She will get her feet wet!'

But Miss Morland did want to go that way, so they set off down the narrow, winding path, through a thick grove of old fir trees. Catherine was struck by its delightfully gloomy look and was glad the General had excused himself and gone off to inspect his cabbages, so she could be alone with her friend.

'I am particularly fond of this spot,' said Miss Tilney, as they picked their way along the path. 'It was my mother's favourite walk.'

Catherine was interested. She had not heard Mrs Tilney mentioned in the family before and was keen to know more.

'I used to walk here so often with her,' her friend continued. 'Though I did not love it then as much as I love it now. Her memory has made it very special to me.'

And yet General Tilney had described the path as cold and damp! Catherine was intrigued. If his wife loved the walk so much, should not the husband love it too? Did it not indicate a certain coldness in his character that he wished to avoid it?

But she kept these thoughts to herself. 'The loss of your mother must have been very painful for you,' she said gently.

'Yes,' said Miss Tilney in a low voice. 'I was only

thirteen, almost too young to know what a loss it would be. I have no sister, you know, and though Henry – ' she stopped and corrected herself ' – though *both* my brothers are very kind, I am often alone.'

Catherine's heart swelled with sympathy for her friend. 'You were with her, I suppose, to the last?'

'No.' Miss Tilney sighed. 'I was away from home at the time. Her illness was sudden and short and before I got back it was all over.'

What? Could it be possible? Catherine's blood ran cold. A husband who disliked the walk his wife had loved so much – and a wife who died so suddenly and unexpectedly! Had the General really cared for Mrs Tilney at all? What had really happened to the poor lady while her daughter was away from home?

She did not, of course, voice any of these horrid suspicions to her friend, but instead asked gently: 'Is there a picture of your mother in the Abbey, Miss Tilney? I would very much like to see it.'

'Yes,' said Miss Tilney. 'It was intended for the drawing room, but my father was unhappy with the painting, so it hangs in my mother's own room now, the one in which she died.'

A portrait of a departed wife, not treasured by the husband! *Here was more evidence,* thought Catherine, *that all was not as it should be at Northanger Abbey.*

'I would be happy to show it to you, if you like. It is a beautiful portrait and, I believe, a very good likeness.'

Catherine said she would like to see it very much, so Miss Tilney led her back into the Abbey and up the main staircase. At the top they turned away from the corridor which led to Catherine's room and entered a long gallery she had not seen before. It was most handsomely fitted up, with many fine portraits and windows that looked out over the countryside, and it ended in a pair of folding doors, which Miss Tilney threw open and quickly passed through. Catherine followed, and found herself in a long corridor, rather dark and gloomy, with another smaller staircase winding downwards to a part of the Abbey she had not seen. Miss Tilney walked on, heading towards a heavy wooden door at the end which was ornamented with rich carving and remained firmly shut. *This was the door,* thought Catherine, her heart beating fast, *the door which led to Mrs Tilney's room! What secrets lay behind it? What story would it tell?*

But, as Miss Tilney reached out her hand to open it, she was stopped by an angry voice from the end of the corridor: 'Eleanor! Where are you going? Has Miss Morland not seen enough?'

It was the General. Whatever was behind that door, he was clearly determined that Catherine would not see it.

Chapter 4
The House at Woodston

Miss Tilney was looking uncomfortable. 'My father only wanted me to answer a note,' she said afterwards, when Catherine asked why her father had called her away just as they were about to go through the mysterious door. 'And he was concerned that you might be tired after our walk.'

They had finished their evening meal, and when the time came for the young ladies to retire to bed, General Tilney announced that he had some letters to write and would be staying up late. Now, alone in her room, preparing for bed, Catherine felt suspicious. To stay up late, hours after everyone else had gone to bed, just to write some letters? It did not sound very likely! *There must be some deeper reason,* she thought, *something that could only be done while the rest of the household was asleep ...*

And then it hit her. Could it be that Mrs Tilney had not died at all? That she was actually alive, here in the house, locked up somewhere as a prisoner and waiting for her husband to bring her nightly supply of bread and water? Was that the secret that lay behind the mysterious door? The idea was shocking, but all the evidence was there: the suddenness of the lady's supposed illness; the absence of her daughter (and probably, decided Catherine, her other children too) at the time; General Tilney's anger when Eleanor was about to take her through the door. It was all so like something out of one of Catherine's beloved books – it had to be true!

It was up to her, she decided. She, Catherine Morland, would find out the truth, uncover the terrible secret of Northanger Abbey and save Eleanor's mother from whatever horrid fate she endured at the hands of her husband. She would be a true heroine just like those in her stories!

But all heroines need rest, especially after so much excitement, and the moment her head touched her pillows, our heroine fell asleep.

* * *

The next day an announcement from General Tilney drove all Catherine's heroic plans from her mind. They were to visit Mr Tilney at his house in Woodston! A ball itself could not have been more welcome for Catherine than this little excursion, so strong was her desire to visit the village and see Mr Tilney there, in his own house. Her heart was bounding with joy when she and Miss Tilney set off in the carriage with General Tilney. To Woodston!

After an agreeable drive of about twenty miles, they entered the village. The General made so many excuses for the dullness of the countryside and the smallness of the village that Catherine was almost ashamed to say how charming she thought it. But in her heart she preferred it to any place she had ever been before and looked in great admiration at the pretty cottages and the neat row of shops. She was so impatient to see Mr Tilney's house that the carriage had arrived before she knew it and then – there he was, waiting for them on the doorstep with a large Newfoundland puppy playing at his feet.

Catherine's mind and heart were too full when they entered the house to observe a great deal, so that when called upon by General Tilney for an opinion, she had very little idea of the room they were sitting in. Upon looking around, however, she immediately saw that it was the most comfortable room in the world.

'It is the prettiest room I ever saw!' she said. 'The prettiest in the world!'

The General looked satisfied. 'We could not compare it to Northanger, of course, or Mr Allen's house at Fullerton,' he said. 'But it is decent enough, and habitable.' And then he turned to Catherine with a meaningful smile. 'It wants a lady's touch to make it perfectly comfortable, of course, do you not agree, Miss Morland?' Another smile. 'And who knows,' he continued, 'but that lady may be with us now ... '

Catherine was probably the only one of the party who did not understand him.

'Oh no, General Tilney!' she said. 'This room needs no improvement! It is quite perfect as it is! Look at the view from the window! What a sweet little cottage there is among the trees – apple trees too! Oh! If this was my house I would never go anywhere else!'

Never did a day pass so quickly! Never was a house so admired! Catherine loved everything she saw: the house, the garden, the village, the meadows that surrounded it ...

And when Mr Tilney announced that he planned to return to Northanger Abbey in a few days' time, her happiness was complete.

Chapter 5
Through the Door

'*Eleanor!*'
It was the end of the next day and Miss Tilney had agreed to show Catherine her mother's room. Again they had passed through the folding doors at the end of the long gallery into the passage beyond, again her hand was upon the handle of the door, and again that same angry cry resounded down the passage:

'*Eleanor!*'

Catherine, hardly daring to breathe, turned to see the dreaded figure of the General at the far end of the gallery. Her first instinct was to hide, but it was too late for that – he must have seen her – and when her friend, with a look of apology, darted past her and disappeared with him, she stood there for a moment, rooted to the spot and unsure what to do.

Catherine looked at the forbidden door. Dare she open it herself and go in? It would perhaps be better if she explored it by herself, without putting her friend at risk of her father's anger again. She did not know what she hoped to find. Some clue to Mrs Tilney's life, perhaps: a letter, or a diary – some proof of the General's cruelty and his wife's unhappy fate. Catherine had read books where unfortunate daughters and unwanted wives had been imprisoned in attics and cellars and crypts and was determined to find out if this had happened to poor Mrs Tilney. How grateful Miss Tilney would be to see her mother again! How impressed Mr Tilney would be by her bravery!

She reached out a hand. The door was not locked. It opened silently and Catherine tiptoed in.

She stopped. She was in a large, well-proportioned room, with a handsome bed, a polished wardrobe, several neatly painted chairs and three long windows that looked out over the grounds and through which streamed the last rays of the afternoon sun. Over the fireplace was the portrait of a very lovely woman in a blue dress who looked out of the painting at Catherine with a little half-smile on her face.

'What are you doing in my room?' she seemed to be saying, more amused than angry. 'Who *are* you anyway?'

Catherine was ashamed. Whatever she had expected to find, it was not this: a perfectly ordinary, pleasant room, as clean and pretty and cheerful as any other. She felt sick. She was tired of exploring and all she wanted was to be back in her own room, safe in the knowledge that nobody knew what she had done.

She was on the point of retreating as softly as she had entered when the sound of footsteps made her pause. To be found here, even by a servant, would be unpleasant, but to be found by the General (who always seemed to appear when he was least wanted) would be much, much worse. She listened. The sound had stopped, and so, determined not to lose a moment, she went back out through the door and closed it quietly behind her.

At that instant, as she stood listening in the passageway, she heard a door below open suddenly, followed by footsteps coming quickly up the stairs, the stairs she would have to pass before she could get back to the gallery. She was trapped, and stood there, rooted to the spot without the power to move, her eyes fixed on the staircase as the footsteps got closer and closer and then—

'Mr Tilney!'

It was true. Mr Tilney was standing at the top of the stairs, slightly out of breath and staring at her in amazement.

'How did you get here?' she said. 'I thought you were – I mean – how came you up that staircase?'

'How came I up that staircase?' he replied. 'It is the quickest way from the stableyard to my room. Why should I not come up it?'

Catherine blushed. She could say no more.

'And may I not, in my turn,' he added, as he pushed open the folding doors into the gallery, 'ask how you came to be here? This passageway is a strange route to take between the main rooms of the house and your bedchamber!'

Catherine looked at the floor. 'I have been to see your mother's room,' she said.

'My mother's room!' said Mr Tilney. 'Why? Is there anything extraordinary in there?'

'No.' Catherine was still unable to look at him. 'Nothing at all.' Then, quickly: 'I thought you did not mean to come back till tomorrow, Mr Tilney. Is it not very late? I must go and change for dinner.'

'I was able to get away earlier than I thought.' Mr Tilney fixed her with a look. 'You look pale, Miss Morland,' he said. 'I am afraid I alarmed you by running up the stairs.' Then, as they began to walk back up the gallery: 'My mother's room is pleasant, is it not? It always strikes me as one of the most comfortable in the house, and I rather wonder that Eleanor should not take it for her own. She sent you to look at it, I suppose?'

'No.'

'It was entirely your idea?'

Catherine was unable to speak. After a short silence, Mr Tilney added, 'I suppose Eleanor has talked about my mother a great deal?'

'Yes,' said Catherine. 'That is – no, not so much. But what she did say was very ... interesting.' She hesitated. 'The way you lost your mother so suddenly, when none of you were at home – and your father, I thought, perhaps had not been so very ... fond of her ... ' Her voice trailed away.

'And because of this,' he replied, his eyes fixed on hers, 'you suspect him of neglect? Or – ' he hesitated, as if he could not believe what he was about to say, ' – something ... *worse*?'

Catherine raised her eyes towards him more fully than she had ever done before. Her cheeks were burning hot.

Mr Tilney took a deep breath. 'My mother's illness,' he continued, '*was* very sudden. She fell ill with a fever while Eleanor was away. As soon as my father realized it was serious he called a doctor who stayed here at the Abbey and was at my mother's side for the full five days of her illness. As was I, as was my brother (*we* were both at home, Miss Morland). As was my father.' He took a deep breath and then continued. 'My mother died on the fifth day, before poor Eleanor could get back.'

'But your father!' Catherine burst out. 'How did he react? Was he much ... grieved by her loss?'

'For a time, greatly so.' They walked on in silence for a few moments. 'My father reacted like the loving husband he was, Miss Morland. I know he is not the easiest of men, and my mother often found his temper difficult to bear. But you are wrong in supposing him not attached to her. He loved her, I believe, as well as it was possible for him to do so.'

'I am glad,' said Catherine. 'It would have been very shocking if – ' She broke off, unsure of what she was going to say.

'If what?' Mr Tilney stopped suddenly in the middle of the gallery and turned to fix Catherine with a look of such frank astonishment that she had to look away. Outside the windows the evening sun was casting long green shadows across the fields and somewhere a bird was singing. 'My dear Miss Morland, if I have understood you correctly, you have formed a notion of such horror that I have no words – ' He broke off and gave his head a little shake. Then: 'Consider the dreadful nature of your suspicions, Miss Morland! The events described in your stories do not really happen! Not in real life, not now, in this century, at Northanger Abbey! We are respectable, rational people who treat each other with kindness and compassion! And we have laws against such horrors!'

Catherine knew that now, of course she did. In a way she always had. But it made no difference. Nothing would ever make up for what she had done, for the way she had entered Mrs Tilney's room without consent, for the dreadful things she had imagined about the General. Mr Tilney was looking at her more kindly now, but his kindness was almost more difficult to bear. He smiled sadly and shook his head. 'Oh my dearest Miss Morland,' he said, 'what thoughts have you been having?'

They had reached the end of the gallery now and, with tears of shame pouring down her face, Catherine ran off to her room.

Chapter 6
News

Our heroine went down to dinner that night with a broken heart. Her dreams of romance were over and she hated herself more than she could say. How could she have imagined those dreadful things about General Tilney? It was not just that he was her host, the master of Northanger Abbey; he was the father of the man whose good opinion she cared about more than anything in the world. The man who – she thought – had once or twice shown her something like affection, but who must now despise her forever. What would she say when she saw him again? What would he say to her?

When Mr Tilney finally appeared, a little late, having been out walking in the grounds, Catherine looked at her hands, her feet, the floor, the wall, anywhere but at his face. But he said nothing, he made no mention of what had happened at all. In fact, the only difference in his behaviour was that he paid her rather more attention than usual and spoke to her with particular kindness. Catherine began to hope that perhaps, just perhaps, her foolishness had not cost her Mr Tilney's entire regard. She felt so thankful that she decided to be a better person from that moment on. She would never again allow herself to be influenced by the stories she read, no matter how charming and entertaining she found them. It was as Mr Tilney had said: they were just stories!

* * *

The next morning, Mr Tilney came in to breakfast with a letter that had just arrived for Catherine.

She had been expecting to hear from Isabella, as she had written to her several times and received no reply, but when she looked at the envelope she saw it was not from her friend in Bath. It was from her brother, James.

Dear Catherine, she read. *I think it is my duty to tell you that everything between me and Miss Thorpe is over.*

What? Surely this could not be true!

I left her and Bath yesterday, she read, *never to see either again.*

'Miss Morland?' said Mr Tilney. 'Is everything all right?'

'It is not bad news from Fullerton, I hope?' said Eleanor. 'Mr and Mrs Morland – your brothers and sisters – I hope none of them are ill?'

Catherine swallowed the lump that was rising in her throat, but she could not stop the tear that fell on the letter she held in her hand. She brushed it away quickly.

'No. No, I thank you,' she said. 'It is from my brother.' She turned back to the letter.

You will hear the facts of the matter soon enough, and

who is to blame. All I can say, my dearest Catherine, is that I hope your visit to Northanger Abbey will be over before Captain Tilney announces their engagement.

Captain Tilney? Could it be true? The young woman Catherine had thought was her friend had deserted her brother and become engaged to *Captain Tilney*? She read on:

After our father's consent had been so kindly given, this is a heavy blow. She has made me miserable forever.

Oh, James. Catherine's cheeks burned with fury at Isabella's behaviour and her heart ached for the poor brother who had loved the faithless girl so much.

It is her dishonesty that hurts the most. Till the very last moment, she told me she was as fond of me as ever and laughed at my fears, whilst all the time ...

How could she? How could she!

Let me hear from you soon, dear Catherine; you are my only friend. And oh, my dearest Catherine, beware how you give your heart ...

And so the letter ended. Catherine looked up to see the two faces across the table regarding her with kindness and concern.

'Miss Morland ... ?' Eleanor hesitated. *'Catherine?'*

'I do not think I shall ever wish for a letter again.'

'My dear Miss Morland.' Mr Tilney got up and went over to the window to look out at the grounds. 'If I had suspected the letter contained such unwelcome news I would have given it to you with very different feelings.'

'It contains something worse than anybody could ever suppose.' A tear ran down Catherine's face. 'Poor James is so very unhappy.'

Henry turned to look at her. 'To have so kind-hearted and affectionate a sister must be a comfort to him,' he said.

'I have one favour to beg of both of you,' said Catherine. 'If your brother is planning to come here, will you let me know, so I may go away?'

'Our brother!' said Eleanor. 'Frederick? What has he to do with your brother's unhappiness?'

'I ... cannot say,' said Catherine. 'But something has happened that would make it very dreadful for me to be in the same house as Captain Tilney.'

The brother and sister looked at each other.

'And your friend Miss Thorpe?' Mr Tilney sat down in the empty chair next to Catherine. 'Am I wrong to suppose that she has a part to play in this sorry tale?'

Catherine looked up at his face then turned away quickly. There was no point in hiding it from them. She nodded miserably.

'You have guessed it, Mr Tilney. Isabella has deserted my brother and is to marry yours. No wonder she has not replied to my letters!'

'I am very sorry for Mr Morland,' said Mr Tilney, carefully. 'Sorry that anyone you love should be unhappy. But –' and here he looked across the table at his sister again ' – I am most surprised at the news of Frederick *marrying* her.'

'It is true, though.' Catherine indicated the letter. 'James says they are engaged.'

'What of Miss Thorpe's family?' said Eleanor. 'Are they ... wealthy?'

Catherine shrugged. 'Not very,' she said. 'I do not believe Isabella has any fortune at all. But that will not matter in your family!' she added. 'Your father told me the other day that he only valued money when it allowed him to promote the happiness of his children.'

Her friends said nothing.

'Is that not true?' Catherine could not believe it. 'You think your father will oppose the marriage because Isabella is *poor*?'

This time, the look between the brother and sister told her everything she needed to know.

* * *

The next day, General Tilney found himself obliged to go to London for a week and Mr Tilney was called away to Woodston, leaving the two girls alone at Northanger

Abbey. Although Catherine was sorry to say goodbye to Mr Tilney, she knew it would not be for too long and, in spite of her concern for James, the time passed in great happiness. The two young ladies were free to walk when they liked and talk as they liked and their friendship increased with every passing day. Catherine confided her feelings about Mr Tilney (and was amazed to discover her friend was not in the least surprised) and Eleanor (for they were now on first-name terms) in her turn told Catherine about a certain gentleman who was both handsome and kind and with whom she had been exchanging letters ever since they met last winter.

'And General Tilney?' Catherine wondered if her question was a little bold, but could not help herself. 'Will he approve the match?'

Eleanor smiled. 'If the time comes that his permission is needed,' she said, 'the gentleman concerned has a large enough fortune to satisfy even a man of my father's ambition.'

Catherine was delighted that her friend had formed an attachment to a man who seemed worthy of her affection (and of whom her father would approve!) and the days passed so quickly that she barely missed Mr Tilney at all. In fact, if it were not for the knowledge that she would one day have to leave Northanger Abbey, our heroine's happiness would have been complete.

How was she to know that day was to arrive so much sooner than she thought?

Chapter 7
The Departure

'My dear Catherine – ' Eleanor's cheeks were pale and her manner greatly agitated. 'I cannot bear it. I come to you on such an errand ... '

It was the third evening after Mr Tilney's departure to Woodston. Catherine and Eleanor had been enjoying themselves so much after dinner, talking and laughing and sharing secrets, that it was past eleven o'clock before they went up to bed. They had just reached the top of the stairs when they had heard the sound of a carriage driving up to the front door.

'Goodness!' Eleanor had cried. 'Who can that be, at this hour?'

The friends looked at each other and the same thought dropped into each of their minds:

Captain Tilney ...

While Eleanor hurried downstairs to greet the new arrival, Catherine had walked on to her room, wondering what she would say to Captain Tilney. She hoped he would not mention Isabella but decided that whatever he said, she would behave in the dignified yet distant manner that befitted a true heroine.

And then came the knock on the door of her room.

'Eleanor?' Her friend came in and stood there for a

moment, trembling and unable to speak.

'What is it?' said Catherine. 'Has something happened?'

'How shall I tell you? Oh, Catherine!'

A new and terrible idea darted into Catherine's mind. Her heart clenched. 'It is a messenger from Woodston!' she cried. 'Henry? Is he hurt?' Both she and her friend were too upset to notice that this was the first time she had spoken his first name aloud.

'No, no,' said Eleanor. 'It is no one from Woodston.' She took a deep breath. 'It is my father, Catherine. He has returned from London.'

'Your father?'

'Oh, Catherine, you are too good, too kind, to think ill of me for what I have to say. After what has lately passed between us, how joyfully, how happily, the time we have spent together—'

'Believe me, Eleanor, I will never think ill of you.'

'Then I will say it.' Eleanor looked her friend straight in the eye. 'My dear Catherine, we are to part.'

'What?'

'My father has remembered an engagement that takes the whole family away on Monday. We are to go to Lord Longtown's for a fortnight.'

'On Monday! But that is only three days away!' Then, seeing her friend's unhappy face: 'My dear Eleanor, do not be distressed. I am very, very sorry we are to part, so soon and so suddenly, but I am not offended. I can finish my visit here another time – or you can come to see me at Fullerton.'

Eleanor's cheeks flamed red. 'I fear that will not be possible.'

'Well, then ... ' Catherine's mind was racing and her heart was beating fast. 'Monday is not so very soon! I need not leave until just before you do. My father and mother do not need to be told I am coming, and the General will send a servant with me, I dare say, for half the way. Then, I shall soon be at Salisbury and from there it is only nine miles to my home!'

'Ah, Catherine! If only it was so! But – how can I tell you? You are to leave tomorrow morning. The carriage will be here at seven and no servant will be offered to accompany you.'

Catherine sat down, breathless and speechless.

'Dear Catherine, I hope you will forgive me.' Eleanor's eyes were full of tears. 'This is my father's wish, not mine. I have no say in his decision.'

Catherine took a deep breath. 'Have I offended the General?' she said.

'Alas! Catherine, I can see no cause for his behaviour. He is certainly very agitated; I have rarely seen him more so. But it cannot be because of you! How could it be?'

'I am very sorry if I have offended him,' said Catherine. Then, seeing her friend's face: 'Do not be unhappy, Eleanor. The journey is nothing.'

'A journey of seventy miles, to be taken on your own, at your age! Oh, Catherine, what will your father and mother say? What will they think of us?'

'Do not think of that now, Eleanor. If we are to part, a few hours sooner or later makes no difference. I can be ready by seven.'

Eleanor saw that she wanted to be alone and so left her, with one last sorrowful look. 'I shall see you in the morning.'

While her friend was there, Catherine had managed to control her tears, but now she was alone they burst out in a torrent. Turned from the house, and in such a way, with no reason, no apology, no explanation! And no chance to say goodbye to Henry! Who could say when they might meet again?

Or if they ever would?

Chapter 8
Home

'Catherine? Can it really be you?'

A heroine returning to her home village at the end of an adventure ought to be a noble and impressive sight: a fine carriage, a multitude of servants, smiling villagers lining the street to witness her triumphant return, her proud family waiting outside the house to greet her ...

How different it was for poor Catherine.

After a troubled night, she had got up that morning at six o'clock to pack her things and eat her last meal at Northanger Abbey. She had hoped the General might relent, and apologize for the rude way he was sending her away, but he did not even appear at breakfast to say farewell.

And of course, there was no Henry.

When the time came for her to leave and the carriage was at the door, Catherine paused a moment, unable to go without some mention of his name, and after she had kissed her friend was just able to ask her in a whisper to pass on her 'good wishes to – Mr Tilney.'

Eleanor nodded and, unable to control her feelings any longer, Catherine hid her face in her handkerchief, jumped into the carriage and in a moment was driven away from the door.

And so the long journey passed, with our heroine weeping and waiting and finally longing to be home.

* * *

'Catherine!'

Our heroine's younger brother George was the first to see the carriage pull up outside the house, but her mother and father and all her other brothers and sisters were soon gathered at the door to welcome her and delight in her unexpected return. But Mrs Morland soon noticed her daughter's pale face and unhappy looks and Catherine was obliged to explain the reasons for her sudden departure from Northanger Abbey.

'This is a very strange business,' said her mother, with a look across the room to Mr Morland. 'And the General must be a very strange man.'

Everyone was of the same mind: General Tilney had acted without honour, kindness or good manners, and Mrs Allen (who had come over as soon as she heard of Catherine's return) spoke for them all when she repeated: 'I really have no patience with the General. No patience at all!'

Nobody guessed there could be any other reason for Catherine's sad looks and loss of spirits. She was not her old self, they agreed, but this was simply a result of the long journey she had endured on top of the General's rudeness.

They never once thought of her heart.

Chapter 9
A Letter

The next morning brought an unexpected letter from Isabella:

My dearest, sweetest Catherine,

I received your kind letters with great delight and send a hundred thousand apologies for not answering them sooner ...

Catherine was in no mood for Isabella's nonsense and read on with increasing impatience.

You know, my Catherine, that you are dearer to me than I can say and I know I can trust you when I tell you that I am quite uneasy about your dear brother ...

What?

I have not heard from him since he left Bath and am fearful of some misunderstanding ...

Misunderstanding? She became engaged to another man!

I would write to him myself but have lost his address in Oxford, and am hoping that your kind intervention may put things right between us. Pray write to him, sweetest Catherine! He is the only man I ever did or could love and I trust you, as his sister and my dearest friend, to convince him of it. The new spring fashions are in the shops, the hats more hideous than you can imagine ...

So Eleanor and Henry had been right. Their father had refused to consent to a marriage between Isabella and their brother (if marriage had ever been that gentleman's true intention!) and Isabella was now trying to revive her engagement with James. Well, she had asked the wrong person to act on her behalf! James would never hear Isabella's name mentioned by her 'dearest, sweetest' friend again. Catherine tore the letter up and threw the pieces on the fire, hot tears of anger stinging her eyes. She was ashamed of Isabella and ashamed of herself for ever having admired her. How could James have fallen in love with such a woman? How could *she* have trusted her, treated her as a friend, loved her even? She would never trust anyone again!

* * *

And so the days passed in silence and in sadness. Mrs Morland watched her daughter with increasing concern. Catherine could neither sit still nor keep busy for more than ten minutes at a time. Nothing seemed to interest her. Nothing could distract her from the languor and listlessness into which she had sunk. All Catherine could think was *now* Henry must have arrived at Northanger; *now* he must have heard of her departure; *now* they were all setting off on the visit to Lord Longtown ...

For two days, Mrs Morland said nothing, but when a third night's rest had neither restored Catherine's cheerfulness nor given her a greater inclination for needlework, she could stay silent no longer.

'I hope you are not fretting about General Tilney,' she said, when she came upon her daughter with her sewing lying neglected in her lap again. 'Because that would be very simple of you. Ten to one you will never see him again.'

Catherine said nothing.

'Catherine?'

Still nothing, so after a short silence, her mother continued gently: 'And I hope, my Catherine, you are not getting out of humour with home because it is not so grand as Northanger Abbey. That would be turning your visit into an evil indeed.'

'I am sure I do not care about being grand. It is all the same to me.'

Mrs Morland looked at her. Then she had an idea. 'Your sister Sarah has got a new book, I believe,' she said. 'It is by the author you admire so much, the lady who wrote *The Mysteries of Udolpho*.'

Catherine picked up her sewing. She did not want to be reminded of her foolishness at Northanger Abbey. She did not want to be reminded of Northanger Abbey at all.

'I will look it out for you,' her mother said, getting up

to leave the room. 'I am sure it will do you good.'

Catherine tried to concentrate on her sewing. A few minutes passed while she sighed, looked at her work, looked at the wall, stared into the fire. When there was a knock at the front door, she did not move. It would be Mrs Allen again, she was sure, come to drink tea, ask after James and show off her new gloves. She did not look round when she heard the door open and two sets of footsteps enter the room. And then, her mother's voice:

'Catherine?' she said. 'We have a visitor, my dear.'

Only then did Catherine look up and see him, standing in the doorway, as her mother said his name:

'Mr Henry Tilney.'

Chapter 10
A Visitor

Our heroine could not speak. Wrapped up in her own unutterable happiness, Catherine listened without really hearing as Henry apologized to her mother for his unexpected appearance, expressed his shock at learning of Miss Morland's sudden departure from Northanger Abbey and his impatience to know that she had arrived home safely. He answered Mrs Morland's polite enquiries about his journey and the weather, while Catherine – the anxious, agitated, happy, feverish Catherine – said not a word. But her bright eyes and flushed cheeks made her mother hope that this good-natured visit had raised her spirits for a while and convinced her that she should perhaps leave the two young people on their own while she busied herself in the kitchen.

And so the truth was told.

On his return from Woodston, Henry had been met by his impatient father, who informed him of Miss Morland's departure and ordered him to think of her no more. The General, Henry said in reply to Catherine's anxious question, had nothing of which to accuse her, she had done nothing to offend him ...

She was only guilty of being less rich than he had thought.

It was John Thorpe who had misled him first. On seeing his son with Miss Morland at the ball, the General had asked John what he knew about her. Pleased to be questioned by such an important man, and having made up his mind to marry Catherine himself, John had boasted about his connection with the Morlands, describing them as far wealthier than they really were and even saying that, as the great favourite of Mr and Mrs Allen, Catherine was due to inherit their property too.

The General had therefore decided that the innocent, charming and seriously rich Miss Catherine Morland would make a fine wife for his son, and so encouraged his daughter to invite her to Northanger Abbey. It was when he met John Thorpe again on his recent visit to London that John (angry at Catherine's lack of interest in him) had told General Tilney the truth. The Morlands were not wealthy. They were an ordinary family, who lived an ordinary life, in an ordinary village with a great many perfectly ordinary children.

Except for one of them, of course. Their daughter Catherine. She was not ordinary at all.

* * *

Mr and Mrs Morland's surprise at being asked by Henry Tilney for their consent to marry their daughter was at first considerable. It had never entered their heads to suspect that Catherine had formed an attachment while she was away, far less that her affections might be returned, and, as Mrs Morland said to her husband, 'She is such a scatterbrained little thing, she will make a sad and careless young housekeeper, to be sure!' But since they loved her, it soon seemed natural to them that Henry did too, and Catherine's sparkling eyes and glowing cheeks told them all they needed to know about her feelings.

So, after some time had passed and the General's temper had subsided (helped in no small part by the announcement of Eleanor's engagement to the handsome and wealthy suitor she had described to Catherine), he allowed his son to return to Northanger Abbey and gave permission for him 'to be a fool if he wanted to!'

Henry did want to, and so, within twelve months of the day they first met, he and Catherine were married. The sun shone, the bells rang and everybody smiled; Mrs Allen had a new gown for the occasion, Mrs Morland wept only a very few tears, and Isabella was not invited; James shook his new brother by the hand and kissed his sister warmly on both cheeks, all the while with his eye on a charming-looking niece of Mrs Allen's who had accompanied her aunt to the wedding; Eleanor appeared as happy as she had ever been; the children behaved better than expected; and everybody agreed many times over that the bride looked very pretty, the groom seemed a true gentleman, and the day was absolutely perfect.

And so we leave them there in the sunshine: Henry, smiling down at his new bride, and our dear Catherine, at last the heroine of her story with her very own happy ending.